A World Without Failures

Growth Mindset

ESTHER

MAIMA

DAVID

First Printing, 2019
ISBN 978-3-948298-03-6

David was sad. And when David was sad, his cat, Einstein, was sad, too.

Today was one of those days when nothing seemed to be working. Summer was coming, and all his friends could swim, but David couldn't stay above water. Then his soccer team lost the match because he missed the game-winning goal. To top it all off, he made two mistakes on his spelling test.

"If I could make one wish—and have it come true," David said to Einstein, "my wish would be never to make a mistake again. Then everything would be easy and I wouldn't have to fail."

David dozed off on his hammock with Einstein snuggled by his side…and he began to dream…

"Why are you wishing for a world without failure?" asked Einstein.

David freaked out a bit, wondering why his cat was suddenly able to talk. But he answered, "**Because that would be great!** I would not need to take swimming lessons any more. I would do it right on the very first try. And I would be able to solve any puzzle and climb the highest trees without ever falling."

Einstein looked at her watch, nodded and walked away.

"I need to go find Dad and tell him that Einstein just spoke to me," David thought. But when he looked for his dad in the kitchen, he noticed something quite strange. The refrigerator was missing! Now, he really needed to find his dad.

"Maybe he's outside." But when David looked out the window, he saw that the supermarket next door was missing! **"What is going on?"** yelled David.

"Dad," he screamed. David headed down the hallway. Maybe his dad was in the bathroom. He always takes a long time in there.

Just then, David smelled something stinky. Einstein was sitting in the hallway, innocently licking her paw. Right next to her was a big, stinky poop.

"Why did you do that, Einstein?" David didn't expect Einstein to answer, but she did. "The door to the bathroom is closed, and the litter box is inside the bathroom."

"But why didn't you just jump on the doorknob and open the door like you always do?"

"I can't do that. It's too hard."

"What do you mean?" asked David. "It took you a lot of tries, but now you know exactly how to do it. That's **not** a good excuse!"

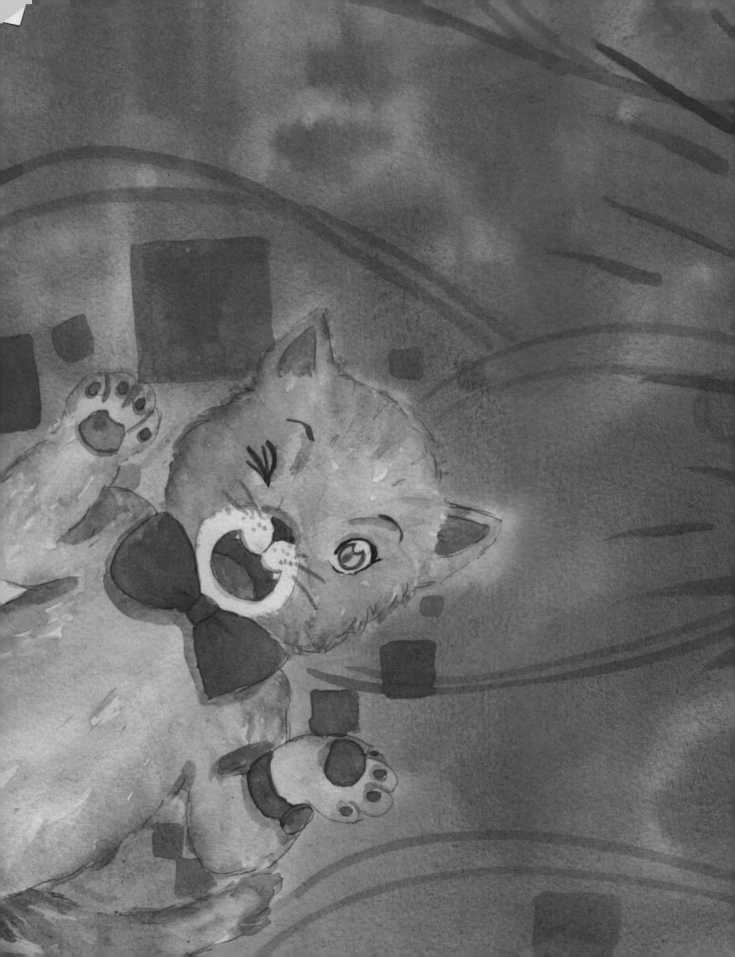

"Don't you remember?" Einstein reminded him.

"We now live in a world without mistakes and failures. If I had tried to open the door, I would have failed many times. This is wonderful, David. Everything is so easy. I don't have to try any more. That was what you were wishing for, right?"

"Is that the reason why the supermarket is gone?" asked David.

"Yes, for sure. That's because nobody could build a supermarket without making a few mistakes. **That would be impossible.**" Einstein seemed to know all the answers.

"And what about the missing refrigerator?"

"Inventing something to keep food cold is pretty complicated. It would never work on the first try. In a world without failure, there would be no refrigerators."

David thought for a second, but nothing seemed to make sense. "Well, Einstein, if that's right, there wouldn't be any TVs either. Don't you think making a TV is also pretty complicated?"

As soon as he said that, the TV disappeared!

"Yes, you are right. There would be no TVs in a world without failures," Einstein said, nodding. David was beginning to feel scared.

"Then maybe there are no houses either?" asked David.
Einstein nodded again, and the house disappeared!

"What about streets?" Just then all the streets were gone.
"Look around," said Einstein. **"This is what a world without
human failure looks like."**

David looked down and saw that his cloths had changed!
Now he was really frightened.

Suddenly, a big lion jumped out of a bush and began to chase David. Running as fast as he could, David tried to get away. Luckily, just before the lion caught him, his dad swung down from a tree and brought him to safety. They waited together in the tree until the lion was gone.

"Where were you, Dad? I was looking for you everywhere. I'm so scared."

"I'm sorry, Son, I would love to spend time together, but I have to go out all day and hunt for our food. In this world, no one could have built a supermarket or a bakery, or pretty much anything."

As it began to get dark, they built a fire to stay warm. David wished for a light switch, but in a world without failure, no one could have invented electricity. It got darker and darker.

Soon it was pitch black. David couldn't remember ever being so scared. "In a world without failure, everything is much harder. This world is hard and scary," David thought to himself.

He closed his eyes. He didn't want to be in this strange world any longer.

David yawned and opened his eyes. Suddenly he was back on the hammock with all his normal clothes. His dad and Einstein were sitting next to him.

"You looked like you were having a very bad dream, Son, so I decided to wake you up," said his Dad. "Are you okay?" Strangely, Einstein didn't say a word.

"Dad, I know I said I wasn't going swimming anymore, but I will keep trying, even though I may fail. I am sure that if I keep trying, I will get it right." David thought,

"Not trying is much worse than failing."

Why is failure often a good thing?

We often think of failure as a bad thing, but what does failure really mean?

- Failure is often just the first attempt at learning something new.
- Failure helps improve your brainpower.
- Failure encourages problem-solving skills.
- Failure helps you become strong and resilient.
- Without failure there is no progress.

It's always better to try and fail then not to try at all.

Discussion Starters

- Other than what you read about in the story, what are some things that would not be possible in a world without failures?
- Share with your child some of the mistakes you have made. Share something from your own childhood and something that happened recently.
- Encourage your child to share something he/she failed to do in the past, but is now able to do. If this exercise seems difficult, try helping with ideas.
- Focus on a growth mindset and think together about things you can't do YET, but soon will be able to do. Be vulnerable and try to share something that is meaningful to you.
- Research together famous people who failed many times, but went on to become very successful. (Examples are Michael Jordan, Albert Einstein, Oprah Winfrey, Walt Disney, Lionel Messi, Eminem, Thomas Edison and The Beatles).

Growth Mindset Book Series

I Can't Do That, YET

A World without Failures

Little Bears Can Do Big Things

Your Thoughts Matter

Download your **FREE Growth Mindset** activity pages here:

free.powerofyet.com/growthmindset

LIKE WHAT YOU READ?

★★★★★

Please leave a review!

I Can't Do That, YET

Enna is a girl who doesn't believe in herself and often utters the phrase "I can't do that!"

One night in a dream she sees all the possible future versions of herself, discovering that she can be any of those versions with time, knowledge and dedication.

She develops a growth mindset throughout her journey and instead of saying "I can't do that," she learns to say, "I can't do that YET!".

A World without Failures

David hates making mistakes. Frustrated and angry at himself for not doing something perfectly the first time, David gets tired of practicing. He wishes for a world with no mistakes, but it's not what he expected.

Without mistakes, the world would have no…
… learning… inventions… growths

After reading this story, children realize that mistakes are a good thing and are important for successful learning.

Little Bears Can Do Big Things

Jimmy and his Dad have a great day planned, until his Dad issues a challenge. He wants the little bear to climb the biggest tree in Beartown, cross a river, and sleep in a cave *all by himself*.

Is it okay for boys to feel afraid? Is it okay for them to need help?

Jimmy shifts his thinking, faces the challenges and is able to make good choices with the help of his friends. He's *even* brave enough to talk about his feelings with his Dad.

Your Thoughts Matter

Romy has two voices in her head; one that causes her to doubt herself, and one that encourages her to keep trying.

Your child's mindset matters, *more than they realize.* Help them understand the power of a **growth** mindset. Told in an engaging way that brings clarity to the subject of mindset, 'Your Thoughts Matter' gives concrete examples of what different mindsets sound like in our heads.
'This is too hard; I'll never learn it.' vs *'It's meant to be hard; we grow by challenging ourselves.'*

Printed in Great Britain
by Amazon